FOR OLIVIA, WITH LOVE BEYOND WORDS
—K.C.

TO JAN AND LENKA D.
—K.L.

For information address HarperCollins Children's Books, a division of HarperCollins Publishers, 195 Broadway, New York, NY 10007.
www.harpercollinschildrens.com
ISBN 978-0-06-257420-6
The artist used mixed media to create the digital illustrations for this book.
Typography by Chelsea C. Donaldson
19 20 PC 10 9 8 7 6 5 4 3

First Edition

I'LL LOVE YOU TILL THE COWS COME HOME

KATHRYN CRISTALDI

KRISTYNA LITTEN

HARPER

An Imprint of HarperCollinsPublishers

I will love you till the cows come home

from a trip to Mars through skies unknown
in a rocket ship made of glass and stone.

I will love you till the cows come home.

I will love you till the yaks come back
from a jaunt downtown for a grassy snack

in a fire truck . . .

or a
Cadillac.

I will love you till the
yaks come back.

I will love you till the sheep set sail

on a cruise ship bound for
the Isle of Kale,

past manatees

and a humpback whale.

I will love you till the sheep set sail.

I will love you till the wolves return
from a bumpy ride over rocks and fern,

the pigs all shouting
with concern.

I will love you till the
wolves return.

I will love you till the frogs ride past

on big-wheeled bikes going superfast . . .

in a circus for sea horses,
shrimp,
and bass.

I will love you till the frogs ride past.

I will love you till the deer dance by
from a tap contest under the blue sky,

with a prize of clover and twig potpie.
I will love you till the deer dance by.

I will love you till the geese flap down

to a warm ski lodge in a snowy town
with gourmet s'mores all chocolaty brown.

I will love you till the geese flap down.

I will love you till the ants march in

wearing tiny ant hats
and tiny ant grins

and birthday cake crumbs on their tiny ant chins.
I will love you till the ants march in.

I'll love you till then, and again and again,
till my love makes a bed for the cows in their pen

and the yaks

and the sheep

and the wolves settle in,

and the frogs softly strum
on their frog violins,

and the deer and the geese and the ants
close their eyes
as the moon sprinkles moon dust
all over the skies.

I will love you till the cows come home,

come home.

I will love you till the cows come home.